A Wiggly, Jiggly, Joggly, Tooth

Written by Bill Hawley
Illustrated by William Joyce

GoodYearBooks

Kevin's tooth was loose.
He wiggled it with his tongue.

He jiggled it with his finger.
He wiggled and jiggled and
joggled it.

His mother said, "Kevin, stop
wiggling that tooth."

His teacher said, "Kevin, stop jiggling that tooth."

His friends said, "Kevin, stop
joggling that tooth."

Kevin didn't listen.
He wiggled and jiggled and
joggled it. And . . .

he swallowed it!